For Jonah and Grandma ~ J C

LITTLE TIGER PRESS LTD,

an imprint of the Little Tiger Group

1 The Coda Centre, 189 Munster Road, London SW6 6AW

www.littletiger.co.uk

First published in Great Britain 2017

This edition published 2017

Text and illustrations copyright © Jane Chapman 2017

Visit Jane Chapman at www.ChapmanandWarnes.com

Jane Chapman has asserted her right to be identified

as the author and illustrator of this work under the

Copyright, Designs and Patents Act, 1988

Printed in China • LTP/1400/1817/0317

2 4 6 8 10 9 7 5 3 1

Love Enough for Two

Jane Chapman

LITTLE TIGER

LONDON

"Mo!" called Grandma one evening.

"I've got a lovely surprise down here!"

"Hoo-hoo! A surprise!" thought Mo.

"I wonder what it could be ..."

He fluttered down excitedly to find out.

Cuddled up in Grandma's wings was a little
bundle of fluff.

"What is it?" asked Mo, peering closer.
The fluffball had two huge eyes and a tiny beak.

"This is your baby cousin, Bibi," whispered
Grandma.

Bibi stared at Mo
and then blinked.

"She's not very chatty," murmured Mo.
Grandma laughed. "Just say 'hi' and
maybe she'll wave – it's her new trick."
"Hi!" smiled Mo.
"Hiya!" cheeped Bibi, wiggling fluffy
feathers at him.

Grandma clapped proudly.

"Who's my clever little honeybun?" she cooed.

"Honeybun?" thought Mo.

"But I'M Grandma's little honeybun!"

"Can Bibi play games?" asked Mo.

"Well, she's very little . . ." chuckled Grandma,

"but I know she'd love to play with a big-boy owl like you."

"What about bunnyhops?" Mo cheeped.

"You play it like this, Bibi . . . Hop! Hop! Hop!"

Mo bounced about like a ping-pong ball, but Bibi was a terrible hopper.

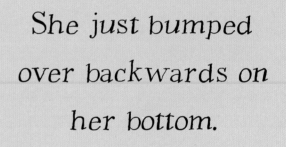

She just bumped over backwards on her bottom.

"Owww!"
she squeaked.

"Poor, precious poppet," soothed Grandma, scooping Bibi up and tickling her tufty tummy till she chirruped with delight.

Mo watched crossly.
"Poor poppet? More like poor ploppet!" he grumped.

"Let's try Bibi in the swing,"
smiled Grandma. "You used to love
it at her age."
"Me first!" called Mo, racing on ahead.

But Mo was too big to fit.
"Big boys need big swings!"
said Grandma. "This one's
for baby owls like Bibi.
Ready, sweetness?"

Mo watched Grandma push Bibi back and forth.
"Look, Mo – Bibi thinks she's flying!" Grandma
hooted. "Would you like to push her?"

But Mo was thinking.
"Bibi likes playing in the swing,
doesn't she? So we can play
hide-and-seek while she's busy!
Start counting, Grandma!"
And he fluttered off.

"Wait, Mo," called Grandma.
"Bibi's too little to play on her own."
    "But I want to play with YOU, not
Bibi!" squawked Mo. "Can't we put
her down for a nap?"
    "Let's have a snack instead,"
said Grandma. "That's something
we can all do together."

Mo flumped on the grass and waited for Grandma to return. "Hiya! Hiya!" waved Bibi, but Mo didn't feel like waving back.

"Snack time!" smiled Grandma, breaking a biscuit in half. "Here's a treat for my two little treasures."

Mo looked down at his half of the biscuit. Suddenly, a tear trickled down his beak and he covered his face to hide his sniffles.

"You used to give me a whole biscuit, Grandma . . ." he cried. "Don't you love me with your whole heart any more?"

"Oh, Mo munchkin!" said Grandma.
"Is that what you've been thinking?"

Grandma sat Mo on her lap for
a snuffly snuggle.

"I've only given you half a biscuit
because it was the last one in the
packet," she explained. "I still
love you as much as ever!"

"But now you've got Bibi . . .
and I'm not little like Bibi
any more," whimpered Mo.

"Well that's true!" laughed Grandma.
"You certainly are a big boy, but no matter
how big you get, you'll always be my
perfect little pickle."

Mo sniffed and cuddled in closer.

"Let me tell you something amazing," Grandma continued. "When a new baby comes along, a grandma grows new love! Bibi hasn't taken away any of my love for you."

"I didn't know that about grandmas," Mo snuffled.

"Better now?" asked Grandma.

But Mo was looking at
his baby cousin.

"Hiya! Hiya!" cheeped Bibi.

She was covered in crumbs from top to toe.

"Oh my! This owlet needs a bath!" laughed Grandma.

"But watch out, Mo – Bibi loves to splash . . ."

"Just like ME!" cheered Mo.
"Come on, Bibi – let's splash Grandma!"

Splish!

Splash!

Splosh!

More books to share with your little poppet . . .

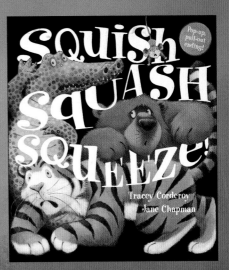

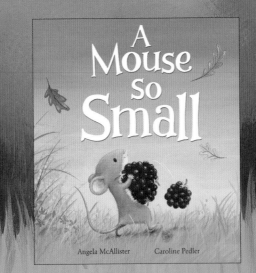

For information regarding any of the above titles or
for our catalogue, please contact us:

Little Tiger Press, 1 The Coda Centre,
189 Munster Road, London SW6 6AW
Tel: 020 7385 6333
E-mail: contact@littletiger.co.uk
www.littletiger.co.uk